Little
White
Rabbit

KEVIN HENKES

Little
White
Rabbit

GREENWILLOW BOOKS
An Imprint of HarperCollinsPublishers

For Greenwillow—then and now

Little White Rabbit. Copyright © 2011 by Kevin Henkes. All rights reserved. Manufactured in China. For information address HarperCollins Children's Books, a division of HarperCollins Publishers, 10 East 53rd Street, New York, NY 10022. www.harpercollinschildrens.com. Colored pencil and acrylic paint were used to prepare the full-color art. The text type is 28-point Tarzana Wide. Library of Congress Cataloging-in-Publication Data. Henkes, Kevin. Little white rabbit/ by Kevin Henkes. p. cm. "Greenwillow Books." Summary: As he hops along, a little rabbit wonders what it would be like to be as green as grass, as tall as fir trees, as hard as rocks, and to flutter like butterflies. ISBN 978-0-06-200642-4 (trade bdg.) — ISBN 978-0-06-200643-1 (lib. bdg.) [1. Rabbits—Fiction. 2. Animals—Infancy—Fiction.] I. Title. PZ7.H389Lit 2011 [E]—dc22 2010011602 10 11 12 13 14 SCP 10 9 8 7 6 5 4 3 2 1 First Edition

Little white rabbit hopped along.

When he hopped through the high grass,
he wondered what it would be like to be green.

When he hopped by the fir trees,
he wondered what it would be like to be tall.

When he hopped over the rock,
he wondered what it would be like
not to be able to move.

When he hopped under the butterflies,
he wondered what it would be like
to flutter through the air.

When he hopped past the cat,
he was too frightened to wonder anything—

so he turned around
and hopped and hopped, as fast as he could.

Soon little white rabbit was home.
He still wondered about many things,

but he didn't wonder who loved him.

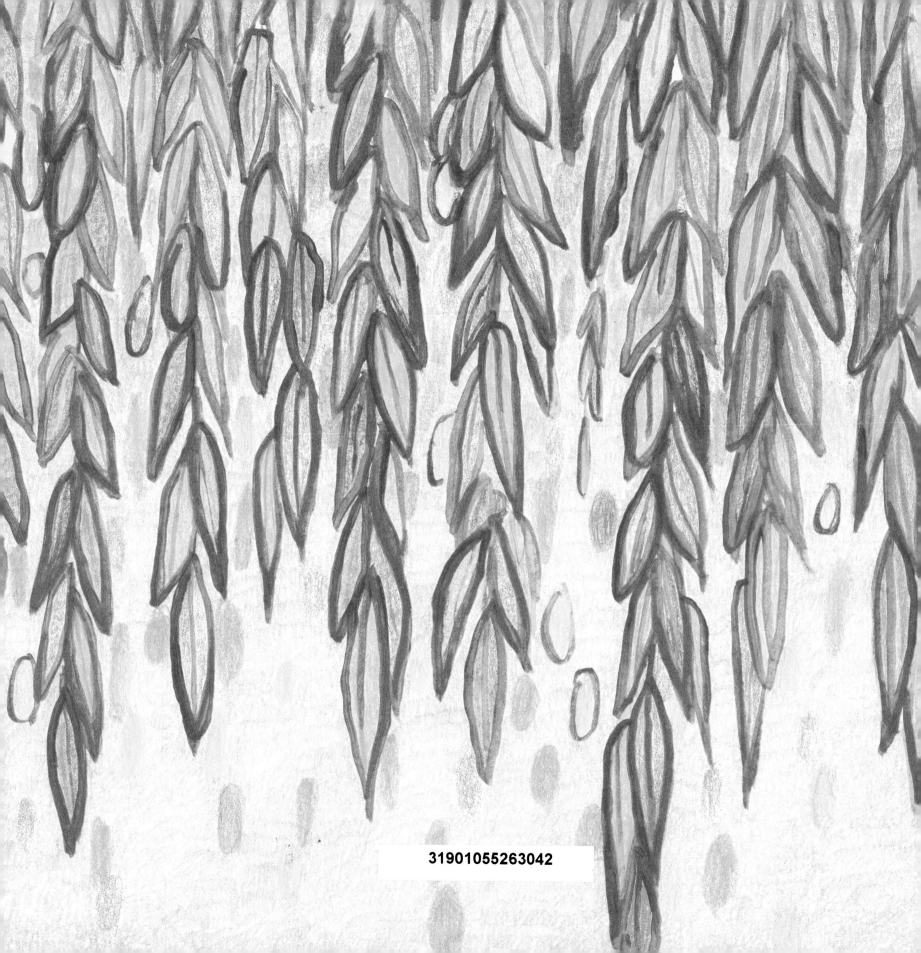